GOBBLE
YOU UP!

Based on a Rajasthani folktale
rendered by Sunita and Prabhat

ART: **SUNITA**

TEXT: **GITA WOLF**

In a large forest...

There lived a wily jackal.

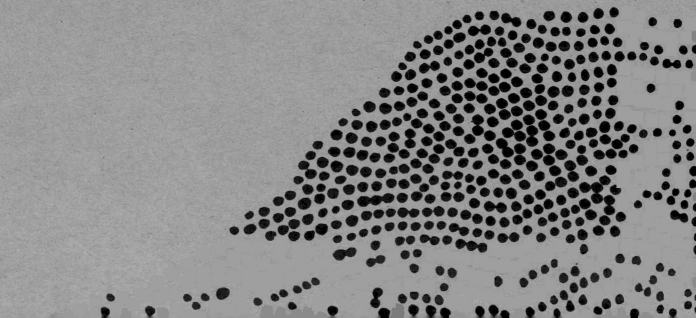

His best friend was a crane.

One day, the jackal was feeling hungry, but he was too lazy to hunt for food.

He was a wily fellow, so he went over to his friend the crane and said, "You're so good at fishing, but I bet you can't catch twelve fish all at once!"

"Twelve? Easy!" cried the crane, and flew straight up.

The crane looked down into the water and sang:

ONE, TWO
THREE FOUR

LET'S SEE
THERE MUST BE MORE

FIVE SIX
SEVEN EIGHT

IN A ROW
SWIMMING STRAIGHT

NINE TEN
ELEVEN TWELVE —

YUM, FISHIES
HOW NICE YOU SMELL!

And **SWOOP!** she caught twelve fish
and laid them down on the edge of the pond.

But what's this? No sooner had she put them down than:

SWISH

SLURP

SMACK

BURRRP!

Before you know it, the jackal gobbled them all up, singing:

**THROUGH THE LIPS
AND OVER THE GUMS**

**WATCH OUT STOMACH!
HERE IT COMES!**

"Oi! That's not fair!" cried the crane. "What about me?"

The jackal was in a fix. He didn't have an answer, so he thought up a quick plan.

He began to sing:

TWELVE FISH
IN MY TUM —

SORRY CRANE,
YOU'RE TOO DUMB!

And **GUUP!** he gobbled up the crane.

A tortoise, who was swimming slowly by, was shocked. "Help!" she shrieked. "I thought you two were best friends!"

The jackal didn't like this at all. He didn't see how it was the tortoise's business.

He dived into the water and SLUUP!
gobbled her up, singing:

TWELVE FISH
IN MY TUM

SORRY CRANE
JUST TOO DUMB —

TA TA, TORTOISE
WHAT A CHUMP!

"Ha, ha, easy with a slow-poke tortoise!" yelled a cheeky squirrel from a nearby tree. "Just try catching me!"

"How dare!" thought the jackal. He was feeling a bit full, but he couldn't let this insult pass.

So he drew in his tummy, took a deep breath, and

WHUM!

he jumped on the tree and gobbled up the squirrel.

"Serves you right!" said the jackal, and sang:

**TWELVE FISH
IN MY TUM**

**SORRY CRANE
JUST TOO DUMB**

**TA TA TORTOISE
GOT NO CHOICE —**

**BYE BYE, SQUIRREL!
STOP THAT NOISE!**

As he came down from the tree, a large cat stood there, staring at him curiously. The jackal didn't like this cat's bulging eyes.

"Speak up!" said the jackal. "Or I'll gobble you up!"

The cat stayed silent, so the jackal had
to keep his word.
BUMM! down she went into his
tummy, and the jackal sang:

TWELVE FISH
IN MY TUM

SORRY CRANE
JUST TOO DUMB

TA TA TORTOISE
GOT NO CHOICE

CHEEKY SQUIRREL
MAKING NOISE —

SPEAK UP, CAT!
LOST YOUR VOICE?

An elegant peacock, passing by, stopped in his tracks.

"My, you've put on weight!" he said, preening his feathers.

The jackal looked down at his own tummy. He was proud of what it could hold.

"I'm not fat!" he yelled, "And if anyone says so, I have to gobble them up!"

And **ZUTHH!** that was the end of the peacock. The jackal sang:

TWELVE FISH
IN MY TUM

SORRY CRANE
JUST TOO DUMB

TA TA TORTOISE
GOT NO CHOICE

CHEEKY SQUIRREL
MAKING NOISE

LISTEN PEACOCK,
FULL OF POISE —

DON'T CALL ME FAT!
I ATE A CAT!

The jackal was feeling a bit heavy by now, so he decided that he could do with a drink of water.

He was just setting off when a huge elephant came lumbering along.

"Hello?" said the elephant, surprised. "You look like an elephant, but where's your trunk? And what happened to your ears?"

This was too much.

"I'm a jackal!" shouted the jackal. "And I'm going to show you by gobbling you up!"

The elephant was a bit hard to swallow, but

DHUMM!

down he went, and the jackal sang:

TWELVE FISH
IN MY TUM

SORRY CRANE
JUST TOO DUMB

TA TA TORTOISE
GOT NO CHOICE

CHEEKY SQUIRREL
MAKING NOISE

PROUD PEACOCK
LOST HER POISE

QUIET CAT
JUST ANNOYS —

GOBBLED YOU UP,
ELEPHANT!

DID YOU REALLY
THINK I COULDN'T?

By now, the jackal's stomach had turned into a
huge balloon.

"No problem, you just need some water," he said
to his tummy. "There's still some space in there."

He swayed slowly to the river, bent down and took a sip of water. It tasted good.

So he took one more sip, then another, and one more, and another... until...

SQUEE! BLEAH! his tummy started making sounds that the jackal had never heard before. He was just about to talk to it sternly when...

BLAMM! his poor tummy finally gave up...
and **BURST.**

Out tumbled everyone, singing:

TWELVE FISH
TUM-TE-TUM

I'M THE CRANE
DUMB-DE-DUM

TA TA TORTOISE
NOW REJOICE

CHEEKY SQUIRREL
MAKING NOISE

PROUD PEACOCK
FULL OF POISE

QUIET CAT
IS OVERJOYED

THE ELEPHANT'S
A BIT ANNOYED —

HA HA, JACKAL!
NOW YOU'RE FOILED!

And the jackal?

He became as thin as a whip.

"I need to find a tailor bird!" he said, as he slank off. "A tailor bird will stitch my tummy up again."

WATCH OUT, WATCH OUT
TAILOR BIRD!

THIS JACKAL'S WILY,
SO WE HEARD.

Originally from Datasooti village in Rajasthan, Sunita was taught to paint by her mother and elder sister.

Called Mandna, this ancient art form is practiced only by women, and kept alive by mothers teaching their daughters how to paint. Intricate designs and flowing images are rendered in white lime on the brown mud walls and floors of village homes. There are no brushes — a piece of cloth soaked in chalk and lime paste is squeezed through the artist's fingers in a fluid line. The art is ephemeral, and renewed regularly, specially during festivals and celebrations. Apart from ritual motifs, one of the favourite themes of Meena artists is animals and their young; village walls team with portraits of all kinds of beasts, wild and domestic.

Meena women usually do not travel outside the confines of their village, and their art is rarely seen away from the original setting. Sunita is an exception, ready not only to explore the wider world, but also to experiment in taking her tradition forward in adventurous ways.

THE MAKING OF **GOBBLE YOU UP**

ORIGINAL IMAGE   PRINTED IMAGE

One of the most striking themes within the Meena repertoire is the pregnant animal, depicted with a baby inside its stomach. It is from this iconic image that the idea for this book originated. Why not construct a tale around an animal within an animal?

We asked Sunita and her husband Prabhat, a Hindi writer, for a story along these lines and Sunita remembered a tale told by her grandfather, about a cunning jackal which swallowed one creature after another. Prabhat wrote down the story that Sunita remembered, and Susheela Varadarajan translated it into English. From the basic plot of the original tale, Gita Wolf wrote the text with cumulative rhyme.

Illustrating the story in the Meena style of art involved two kinds of movement. The first was to build a visual narrative sequence from a tradition which favoured single, static images. The second challenge was to keep the quality of the wall art, while transferring it to a different, and also smaller, surface. We decided on using large sheets of brown paper, with Sunita squeezing diluted white acrylic paint through her fingers.

We photographed Sunita's images, and Production Manager C. Arumugam converted them into flat graphic images that could be printed by silkscreen. In order to draw attention to the sophisticated detailing inherent in Sunita's art, book designer Rathna Ramanathan split the images into two colours. The jackal — the protagonist — is rendered in black, and all the creatures he swallows in white. Gotham, a modern typeface inspired by an architectural vernacular was used as a compliment to the contemporary quality of the art.

The book was printed on kraft paper, specially produced for the project. The paper was cut to a printable page size, printed by silkscreen in two colors, section sewn and hand bound by our team of printers and binders.

Gita Wolf, concept and text
Rathna Ramanathan, design
C. Arumugam, production

FOR ANUSHKA, WHO KNOWS WHY

GOBBLE YOU UP!

Copyright © Tara Books Pvt. Ltd. 2013
www.tarabooks.com

For the illustrations: Sunita

For the text: Gita Wolf, based on a Rajasthani folktale

Design: Rathna Ramanathan, Minus9 Design

Production: C. Arumugam

Printed by T. S. Manikandan, A. Neelagandan, K. Prabu,
A. Arivalagan, T. Sakthivel, R. Shanmugam, S. Mariappan,
P. Siva, A. Ramesh, M. Rajesh, S. Boopalan and S. Chinraj
and bound by M. Veerasamy, Venugopal, S. Manigandan,
M. Vinodha, V. Usha, N. Shanthi, R. Selvi and A. Jayalalitha
at AMM Screens, Chennai, India

ISBN: 978-81-923171-4-4

Many thanks to Susheela Varadarajan, for translating
the Hindi text